Act Normal

And Don't Tell Anyone About

The Dinosaur In The Garden

By Christian Darkin

First Printing 2016 by Rational Stories

www.RationalStories.com

The illustrations are by the author but use some elements for which thanks and credits go to www.obsidiandawn.com, kuschelirmel- stock, Theshelfs and waywardgal at Deviantart.com
Story and illustrations by © Christian Darkin.

CHAPTER 1

This is a letter to me – from me.

Read it and remember it because I think you might be going to forget and you really, really shouldn't.

Dad says you should never eat 5 kinds of sweets and 3 kinds of crisps and 4 kinds of fizzy drinks all at the same time. I didn't think he was right, but he really, really is.

Here is why...

People in this story (I don't think I'll forget this, but just in case):

Me: I am Jenny. I live in England. People often say, "Jenny does things her own way," or, "Jenny thinks outside the box," but I didn't know there even was a box you were supposed to think in, so I don't take much notice.

Sometimes they say, "Jenny isn't normal," and when they start to say that, I just act normal and usually they stop. Acting normal means standing still and smiling. It also means pretending you didn't do whatever strange thing is happening.

I have to do that often because strange things happen to me a lot.

Adam: Adam is my little brother. People often say, "Adam is like a little tank," because when he gets going, you can't stop him and he tends to make a big mess and it looks like he has blown everything up. Adam isn't scared of anything because he doesn't know how to be scared yet. He's not scared of going too high on a swing, or talking to teachers (even the headmistress). He's not even scared of dinosaurs – which is lucky.

Dad: You can't really tell with dad what's good and what's bad. Sometimes he says "No" to things which are really good ideas (like having two puddings instead of dinner). Sometimes he says "Yes" to things which are really bad ideas. (Like keeping chickens. That was a really bad idea). Sometimes he doesn't say anything, but his eyes go really wide and scared looking.

That's when you've told him what really happened and you know he's thinking about what to do next.

CHAPTER 2

We were getting ready to go to Adam's friend's birthday party and I told Dad I wanted to do an experiment. Doing experiments is like cooking, but with dangerous chemicals. Great things always happen when you do experiments, but Dad said, "Dangerous chemicals are hard to get."

But when he was dropping us at the party, Dad also said not to eat too many sweets and crisps and fizzy drinks at the party because "Sweets and crisps and fizzy drinks are full of dangerous chemicals."

The party was in a big hall, and there were lots of little kids, so I helped the grown-ups look after them. They liked that because most of the grown-ups were watching football on the TV in the other room.

One of the grown-ups dressed up as a dinosaur and came in roaring. The little kids all ran away and it chased them. All except Adam. He ran up to the dinosaur and knocked it over. Then all the little kids jumped on it.

That was funny, but it gave me an idea for a plan. All the little kids had got sweets. When they attacked the dinosaur, they all gave their sweets to me to look after so they could hit it harder.

When they had killed the dinosaur, they had all forgotten about the sweets, and had crisps instead.

Then the dinosaur came back, and they all gave me their crisps.

There were also a lot of fizzy drinks and the little kids left them lying around the room. The grown-ups told me to clear them up so they didn't fall over when the dinosaur came back.

I didn't eat the sweets or the crisps. I carefully kept five different kinds of sweets, and three different kinds of crisps in a bag for my experiments. I also kept four different kinds of fizzy drinks but I had to use a plastic bag for them. This was because, I had to hide them in my coat on the way home which made everything in the car a bit sticky.

The next morning I got up before Dad, and did my experiment in the kitchen. I got the crisps and the crunchy sweets and I smashed them all to bits with a shoe. Then I scraped them up and put them in a bowl.

Then I got the softer, sticky jelly sweets and mashed them all together with the fizzy drinks. (There wasn't much left of the fizzy drinks because there was a bit of a hole in my plastic bag). Then I put them in the microwave until they went soft like a kind of slime.

Then I mixed all the crunchy sweets and crisps into the slime. It didn't look very nice, but I knew it must have had lots of dangerous chemicals in, so the experiment was going well.

Just to finish off, I put it all back in the microwave for a really long time. When I got it out, can you guess what it looked like?

CHAPTER 3

Not very nice.

It had gone into crunchy, coloured lumps, a bit like tiny fruit gums - if fruit gums were made of stones.

My experiment was supposed to be a food experiment, but when it was finished I decided not to eat it.

I decided it was probably a chicken food experiment after all.

I put it into three bowls (all good experiments have to be put into three so you know the same things happen when you do it three times). I put the first bowl into the chickens' feed in the garden next to the pond.

We have three chickens, Road-Runner, Big-Bird and Thunder-Bird.

When Dad does food experiments and we don't want to eat them, he always turns them into chicken food experiments, so I thought that was OK. The chickens seemed to like the crunchy crisp sweet fruit gum stones.

I put the other two bowls under my bed because they smelled like burnt marker pens.

The next day, Dad said the kitchen smelled funny and the floor was a bit sticky and crunchy, but I acted normal and he didn't say anything else.

I helped Adam feed the fish in the pond. That's when I got the first idea something bad was happening.

There were no fish in the pond. None. The chickens were being a bit strange. They had eaten all their food. Also, they had eaten their food bowls. Also they had eaten most of the plants, and their bedding, and some of the fence.

Then I saw the chickens. Road-Runner was racing round the garden chasing a big bee. Big-Bird and Thunder-Bird were fighting. Then they stopped and looked at Adam and me.

Then I saw they didn't have beaks anymore. They had big mouths with big spiky teeth. The feathers had fallen off their wings too, and they looked like big claws now.

There was something else that was odd too, but before I could decide what it was, Thunder-Bird said, "Grrr!" at us.

Adam made a louder, "Grrr!" back, because he doesn't know how to be scared.

I do know how to be scared, so I was.

I told Adam to run and we both ran back into the kitchen and slammed the door.

"What's the matter?" said Dad.

"Nothing," I said, and we both acted normal.

"Are the chickens hungry?" said Dad. "Shall I go and feed them?"

"I fed them already," I said. It was true – sort of.

When I looked out of the window, I saw the other odd thing about the chickens. They now had tails. Not little short chicken tails, but long, thin lizard tails.

I could see now what had happened. My experiment had changed the chickens into dinosaurs!

I decided to find out how so I went to my room and asked the Internet and this is what I found...

CHAPTER 4

Inside every bit of every animal is a sort of shopping list (called DNA) to tell it which bits it needs. That's how fish changed into dinosaurs and dinosaurs changed into birds a long, long time ago.

Shopping list for a fish

Head
Eyes
Tail
Fins
gills

Shopping list for a dinosaur

Head
Eyes
Tail
~~Fins~~
~~gills~~
Legs
Big teeth

Shopping list for a chicken

Head
Eyes
~~Tail~~
~~Fins~~
~~gills~~
Legs
~~Big teeth~~
Wings

Dinosaurs aren't chickens because they've got new things on their shopping lists.

The thing is, the old dinosaur stuff is all still there in the chickens. It's just crossed out.

It turns out my experiment just sort of un-crossed it.

That's not good.

I know most kids my age don't ask the Internet this kind of thing. And I know most kids my age don't turn their chickens into dinosaurs. But that's why people say I'm not normal.

While I was in my room, I remembered the other two bowls of experiment. They smelled pretty bad by now. I told Adam to get rid of one bowl, but I kept the other one just in case.

It was tea time when Adam told me how he'd got rid of it and I knew things were going to get worse...

CHAPTER 3

Not very nice.

It had gone into crunchy, coloured lumps, a bit like tiny fruit gums - if fruit gums were made of stones.

My experiment was supposed to be a food experiment, but when it was finished I decided not to eat it.

I decided it was probably a chicken food experiment after all.

I put it into three bowls (all good experiments have to be put into three so you

"Why is that a good place?" I asked.

He said, "Because then the birds can all have some and then they can all be dinosaurs."

I couldn't reach the bowl so Adam had to climb up the tree and get it. He is very good at climbing up trees. He isn't so good at climbing down so he got stuck.

I had to take my shoes off and climb up to help him. My shoes are rubbish for climbing trees in. That's when I saw in the bowl. Most of the experiment was gone.

"Most of the experiment is gone!" I told Adam. "The birds must have eaten it."

"Goody!" he said. Adam put the rest of the experiment in his pocket.

"But now we're in a tree in a dark wood, and the wood is full of dinosaurs," I said.

"Goody!" said Adam. Adam doesn't know how to be scared, but I do.

On the ground I saw a little dinosaur that used to be a robin. It had red feathers and jumped around. Next to it, I saw two more black dinosaurs that used to be blackbirds. They had great big heads.

On the other side of the tree, more little dinosaurs were coming. It was time to go.

"We have to run," I said.

Adam jumped out of the tree. I jumped too. The dinosaurs looked at us. I threw the bowl at them. Then I threw my shoes at them. They got out of the way and we both ran.

The dinosaurs ran after us. They were very fast, but we were fast too. I was fast because I was scared. Adam was fast because he is always fast. Also, he does not stop for bushes or nettles. He just runs into them.

That's why people say he is like a tank.

When we got to the edge of the wood, there were lots of dinosaurs chasing us. There were red ones that were robins and black ones that were blackbirds. There was even a heron one that was very tall and had a long neck and a long mouth full of teeth.

We ran out into the street and just got into the house in time. I could see the dinosaurs outside, snapping their teeth. In the end, they went away.

Dad said, "Were you playing with your friends?"

I said, "Sort of."

Dad said, "Where are your shoes?"

I said, "Isn't it bed time?" and Dad said that it was.

As he tucked me in, Dad said, "Is there something strange happening again? Is it something I should know about?"

I pretended to get very sleepy, and he just patted my head and turned off the light.

The next morning when we came down to breakfast, Dad looked sad.

CHAPTER 6

"I'm afraid the chickens are gone," said
Dad. "I think a fox must have got them."

I looked out of the window. The garden
was a mess. All the plants had been
broken. There were fur and feathers
everywhere.

It didn't look to me like a fox had got
them. It looked like they had got a fox. I
didn't say anything to Dad. I just acted
normal.

"Can we get more chickens?" said Adam,
"Pleeeeeeese..." He did his best sad look.

Dad said, "Yes."

This was Dad saying "Yes" to something that was a really bad idea.

We got in the car and went to the farm. Adam was smiling all the way.

The farm was where Dad had got the chickens, but they had other animals too, and Dad always took us to see all of them.

They had ducks. Adam walked right past the ducks.

They had turkeys. Adam walked right past the turkeys.

They also had pigs, cows, rabbits and ponies. Adam walked right past all of them.

I stopped to look at the ponies and the rabbits, and the pigs. They were all very sweet. But that's when I lost Adam.

Dad was ordering more chickens, so I looked for Adam.

When I found him, I saw the animal he was looking for. I almost cried. I had forgotten the farm had ostriches.

Ostriches! They were huge! They were bigger than me. They were bigger than Dad. And Adam was taking the rest of my experiment out of his pocket and feeding it to them.

This was bad. Very, very bad. If a blackbird could turn into a dinosaur that could chase you home, what would happen to an ostrich?

I grabbed Adam and Dad, and got them back into the car.

"What's the hurry, Jenny?" said Dad.

I didn't say anything, but Adam looked out of the back of the car and giggled all the way home.

CHAPTER 7

I had a very bad feeling by now.

I couldn't look on the Internet until after tea. By then, some strange things were happening. I had some messages from my friends:

Hi Jenny,
I just saw the people from the farm running away from the town. They looked really scared. What is happening? Is this you again?
Sam

Hi,
I can hear roaring coming from the woods.
I'm going to look.

Alfred

Jenny,
Come over to play.
There's a really big footprint in our garden
and we're using it as a paddling pool.

Alison x

I sent a message to everyone:

Dear everyone,
Please don't go outside to play today.
Me and my brother have made some dinosaurs
by mistake.

There are some in the woods and some may have
escaped from the farm.

The ones in the wood will chase you,
but the ones from the farm are probably very big.
Those ones might eat you.

Love from
Jenny xxx

I don't normally put three kisses but today I decided I would. My friends are used to getting messages like that from me, and they know to do what I say.

I decided to call Alfred anyway because he said he was going to the woods. Alfred is a bit like my brother only older, and sometimes he needs you to tell him things more than once.

I called him.

"Don't go to the woods!" I said.

"But you said there were dinosaurs. I like dinosaurs," said Alfred.

"Don't go to the woods," I said.

"OK," he said. "I'll just have a little look."

"Don't go to the woods," I said.

"Don't worry, I won't," said Alfred. "I'll come back straight away."

"Alfred?" I said, "Are you in the woods now?"

"Sort of," said Alfred.

"Oh no!" I said, "Go back home now."

"But there aren't any dinosaurs," he said. Then I heard a really loud roar over the phone. "Oh, those dinosaurs!" he said.

I told him to run. He did run. I could hear a really big dinosaur chasing him, but he told me it couldn't get through the trees so he got away.

Just as he got home, the little dinosaurs came and bit the bum out of his trousers.

"Don't tell your Mum what happened," I said, "or I will get into trouble."

"What shall I tell her?" he said.

"Just act normal," I said.

I told Adam we had to do something, and after Dad put us to bed, we quietly got dressed and crept downstairs. I took my torch. Adam took his Nerf gun and lots of bullets. But they are only made of foam so I didn't think they would help much.

We crept past Dad and went outside. I knew I had forgotten to make something, but I couldn't think what it was.

Luckily there was an important (and very loud) football match on and all the grown-ups were inside their houses, so nobody saw or heard what happened next.

CHAPTER 8

It turns out that big dinosaurs are not very hard to follow even in a town.

They break a lot of things and make a lot of noise. Also, they poo A LOT and their poos are very big and very smelly just like big dogs.

I don't mean big and smelly like big dog poos. I mean big and smelly just like big dogs. They are about the same size as big dogs and about as smelly. They came up to Adam's chest when he jumped in them.

That's how we followed the big dinosaurs
to the supermarket car park. Most of the
cars had been squashed by big dinosaur
feet, and thrown about by big dinosaur
claws.

There were five big dinosaurs. They looked
a bit like T. Rexes, but they had longer
necks and black and white ostrich feathers.
They were also more scary than T.Rexes
because T. Rexes are only ever on TV and in
books.

They had pulled the meat counter out of the shop and they were gulping down whole legs of lamb and whole joints of beef and whole frozen turkeys like ice lollies.

They did not see us.

Not until Adam decided to shoot at them with his Nerf gun. The little bullets bounced off the big dinosaurs' heads, and they turned and roared at us.

Adam roared back at them but he wasn't as loud.

That's when I remembered what I'd forgotten to make when we left the house.

I'd forgotten to make a plan.

I told Adam to RUN. While we were running, Adam said, "We can't just run away all the time."

I knew he was right. We had to think of something to do other than just running. But right now, with five big dinosaurs chasing us, running was the best idea I could think up.

If I could make the Nerf gun fire some kind of poison dart, or if I could change the torch into a laser, that might work. But I couldn't do those things. Not while we were running, anyway.

 We ran as fast as we could. The dinosaurs were faster, but they kept stopping to bite street-lamps and cars and each other.

We ran past the shops and the dinosaurs followed us. We ran through some gardens and the dinosaurs followed us there too. We even ran through the playground and the biggest dinosaur bit a big lump out of the slide.

If you wanted to use the slide now, you'd have to jump the gap on the way down.

We didn't stop to use the slide because the dinosaurs were getting very close. I could hear their teeth going "Snap, snap, snap!" just behind my head.

We were getting very tired, but we saw our front door, and got inside just before the dinosaurs got us. The house was dark because the football match had finished and Dad had gone to bed.

Adam and I were safe, but all the dinosaurs were in the garden. That was really bad. They were making a big mess.

They were thirsty after the long run and they were drinking our pond.

Now was the time to make a plan.

I am quite good at making plans, and I make my best plans when things get really bad.

The plan I made would be a good one if it worked, but it was very dangerous...

CHAPTER 9

I went upstairs to my room and looked under my bed. Luckily Dad hadn't thrown my last bit of experiment away. Do you remember, there were 3 bowls with my experiment in? One was fed to the chickens. Adam took the other one and fed it to the birds in the wood and the ostriches.

I kept the third one just in case.

I decided that "Just in case" was right now.

Adam got all his best tricks. He got his Nerf gun and his football, and his drum. He also took his toy monkey that sang songs really loud (only it sang them in Japanese because it was broken).

He slowly opened the back door and went outside. He tried firing his Nerf gun at the dinosaurs again, but they were drinking from the pond and they didn't take any notice. He tried kicking his football at them but one of them just flicked it with his tail and it went into next door's garden.

He banged the drum and switched on the monkey and the noise was really loud but the dinosaurs just kept drinking. They must have been really, really thirsty.

This was good.

In the end, Adam ran up to one of the dinosaurs and kicked it in the bum.

The dinosaur turned round. Then it got up. Then they all got up. Adam did his best roar. He roared at them all as loud as he could. Then he turned round and ran away round the house. The dinosaurs all followed him, snapping their teeth and roaring.

Adam giggled but he kept running.

When they had gone around the side of the house, I crept out of the back door and I poured my last bowl of experiment into the pond. I had to scrape it out with my finger because it was a bit of a crunchy sticky mess by now, and it had bits growing in it which were furry and smelled really bad.

I washed my finger in the water because I didn't want to turn myself into anything by mistake.

Just then, Adam came running round the side of the house. He was being followed by the dinosaurs. They were snapping and roaring and I would have been very scared if I was him.

I grabbed Adam's hand and pulled him back into the house and we slammed the door just before the biggest dinosaur grabbed us.

They roared and crashed about a bit outside and I think they were quite angry. But in the end they stopped looking for us. They went back to drinking the pond.

The first bit of my plan was working.

We watched out of the window.

Adam said, "What now?"

I tried to tell him what my experiment did. I told him about the shopping lists:

Shopping list for a
fish

Head
Eyes
Tail
Fins
gills

Shopping list for a
dinosaur

Head
Eyes
Tail
~~Fins~~
~~gills~~
Legs
Big teeth

Shopping list for a
chicken

Head
Eyes
~~Tail~~
~~Fins~~
~~gills~~
Legs
~~Big teeth~~
Wings

I told him the experiment sort of un-

crossed out some of the things on the lists

so the birds went back to what birds had

been a long time ago which was dinosaurs. But Adam didn't get it. He's a bit young.

Then, as we watched, a funny thing happened.

First, the big dinosaur's feathers started falling out. Then it started getting smaller. Then its tail started getting short and tall.

Then all the other dinosaurs started changing too.

Their heads got less snappy and their necks got shorter.

They were still drinking, but now they stuck their heads right into the pond. Adam started giggling again. The dinosaurs' legs and arms started to turn into flappy fins, and they got smaller and smaller until one by one, they plopped all the way into the pond and started swimming around.

My experiment had made the birds turn back into dinosaurs. Now, when I gave it to the dinosaurs, it had turned the dinosaurs back into fish!

CHAPTER 10

In the morning, Dad was in a good mood. He was a bit surprised that the garden was such a mess, but then I told him the fish were back in the pond. He was happy about that.

Then he looked at the fish.

I think it would have all been OK if the fish hadn't looked quite so dinosaury. They were sort of green with big hard scales and pointy fins with spiky bits like claws on them.

They didn't really look enough like our old goldfish.

Dad sat me down by the pond.

"Tell me what happened," he said.

Then he gave me the look that says, "Really tell me, and don't act normal."

So I told him.

I told him about the experiment and the chickens and the ostriches, and the dinosaurs in the wood. I even told him we went out hunting them at night, and I knew he wouldn't like that bit.

Then I told him we turned them back into fish, which he did say was very clever.

Then I told him that there were a few little things I hadn't been able to put back to normal. Like the mess in the garden, and the squashed cars at the supermarket, and the little dinosaurs that were living in the wood.

That was when he got that scared look when his eyes go all wide and he doesn't say anything for a long time.

In the end, he said, "I think I'd better tell the Prime Minister."

The Prime Minister runs the country, and you don't talk to the Prime Minister except about really important things. I was a bit scared that I'd get into trouble if everyone knew about the dinosaurs.

But when I got home from school, Dad said he had spoken to the Prime Minister. The Prime Minister had said that England had won the very important football match last night, and everyone was happy, so it would be a pity to make them all sad and scared by telling them about the dinosaurs.

He thought it would be better to just get all the squashed cars taken away, and send some people to catch as many of the dinosaurs in the wood as they could.

I said, "But lots of people saw footprints and broken cars and everyone at the farm would know, and Alfred got chased and they bit his bum."

Dad said that was OK because the Prime minister had people who could use special ray guns to make them forget what they'd seen.

I don't know if Dad really did talk to the Prime Minister, but right now, out of my window I can see some men coming to the door, and one of them has something that looks like a ray gun - so maybe Dad did talk to him after all.

I decided to write all this down anyway just in case I forget about it.

Important things to remember:

1) There probably are still a few dinosaurs in the wood, so you'd better look out if you go playing there.

and

2) Don't eat 5 kinds of sweets and 3 kinds of crisps and 4 kinds of fizzy drinks at the same time.

The End.

Act Normal And Read More

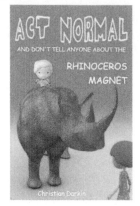

Printed in Great Britain
by Amazon